BERT AND THE

A Sesame Street Start-to-Read Book™

by Sarah Roberts
illustrated by Joe Mathieu

Featuring Jim Henson's
Sesame Street Muppets

Random House/Children's Television Workshop

Library of Congress Cataloging in Publication Data:
Roberts, Sarah. Bert and the missing mop mix-up. (A Sesame Street start-to-read book)
SUMMARY: Ernie's search for a mop turns up some surprising items as his misunderstanding friends try to help.
[1. Puppets—Fiction] I. Mathieu, Joseph, ill. II. Title. III. Series. PZ7.R54428Be 1983 [E] 82-22971 ISBN: 0-394-85752-6 (trade); 0-394-95752-0 (lib. bdg.)
Manufactured in the United States of America   5 6 7 8 9 0

MISSING MOP MIX-UP

One day Bert was painting.

It was hard work.

It made Bert thirsty.

He got out the milk.

SPLAT!

Bert dropped the milk.

"ERNIEEE!" yelled Bert. "Help!"
Ernie came running.
"Bert! Why did you pour milk
on the floor?" asked Ernie.

"I did not POUR it," said Bert.
"I SPILLED it!
   Please go out and find a mop.
   And hurry!"

Ernie ran down Sesame Street.
He saw Betty Lou.
"Bert needs a mop. Do you have one?"
he asked Betty Lou.
"Gee, I don't know," she said.
"But I will look for one."

Betty Lou walked down the street.
"If Bert needs a map,
    he must be going on a trip!"
she said.

"I will look for a map
and ask him to send me
a postcard."

Betty Lou knocked on
Oscar's trash can.
CLANG! CLANG!
"Who woke me up?" growled Oscar.

"I did," said Betty Lou.

"Bert needs a map.

Do you have one?" she asked.

"How should I know?" yelled Oscar.

"I am asleep!"

SLAM! went the lid.

Oscar peeked out of his trash can.
Now he was wide awake.
"If Bert needs a mat,
I will find one," growled Oscar.
"Then maybe everyone will leave
me alone."

Soon Big Bird came along.

"Hi, Oscar!" said Big Bird.

"How are you today?"

"ROTTEN!" yelled Oscar.

"Bert needs a mat.
So I am looking for one,
and I hate helping!"

Big Bird ran home.
"If Bert needs a mitt,
he must want to play baseball!
Maybe I can play too,"
said Big Bird.

Big Bird got his bat
and started to look for a mitt.

Big Bird looked all
around his nest.
He saw no mitt.
But he did see Grover.
"Bert needs a mitt.
Do you have one?"
Big Bird asked Grover.

"I will be so happy
    to look for one!" said Grover.
And he ran home to look.

"Bert needs a mitten!"
Grover told his mother.
"I will help you find one,"
said Grover's mother.
"Oh, good!" said Grover.
"Then Bert will be nice and warm."

Just then Herry came
to Grover's window.
"Come out to play!"
called Herry.
"I can't," said Grover.
"Bert needs a mitten.
I am looking for one!"

Herry smiled to himself.

Then he ran to the pet shop.

"I know how Bert feels,"
Herry said.
"Everyone needs a kitten.
Kittens are so nice!"

Herry picked the nicest kitten.
"You will make Bert so happy!"
Herry told the kitten.
PURRRRR went the kitten.

Bert looked at the clock.

He looked at the puddle of milk.

He tapped his foot.

"Where is Ernie with that mop?"
he said.

Suddenly everyone on Sesame Street
rushed in.
And everyone had something for Bert.

Betty Lou had a great big map.
Oscar had an old, dirty mat.
Big Bird had a baseball mitt.
Grover had a warm woolen mitten.
Herry had a furry little kitten.

Bert looked at the map,

the mat,

the mitt,

the mitten,

and the kitten.

"What's going on?" cried Bert.
"All I needed was a MOP!
And where is Ernie?"

Just then Ernie came home.
"Look, Bert, I found a mop!"
said Ernie.

"You're too late, Ernie,"
said Bert.
"I don't need a mop anymore."
And everyone watched the kitten
lap up all the milk.